Sedric
AND THE
GREAT PIG RESCUE

Angie Morgan

Before I start my story here is some really useful stuff about...

THE ROMANS

A **VERY** long time ago the **ROMANS** came to **BRITAIN**.

They did some fighting and they swaggered about and showed off a lot.

They built huge posh houses called **VILLAS** that had things called **BATHS** in them.

They wore things called **TOGAS** which were basically just **SHEETS**.

They also invented **CENTRAL HEATING** due to it always being **FREEZING COLD** in Britain.

Sedric
AND THE
GREAT PIG RESCUE

First published in Great Britain 2015
by Jelly Pie an imprint of Egmont UK Ltd
The Yellow Building, 1 Nicholas Road, London W11 4AN

Text and illustration copyright © Angie Morgan 2015
The moral rights of the author–illustrator have been asserted.

ISBN 978 1 4052 7528 6

www.jellypiecentral.co.uk
www.egmont.co.uk

A CIP catalogue record for this title is available from the British Library

Printed and bound in Great Britain by the CPI Group

58652/1

MIX
Paper
FSC   FSC® C018306

Lazy Roman person →

spaghetti

(They all got REALLY BAD indigestion from all that eating lying down.)

olives

pizza

They were very lazy and they had all their meals in **BED**.
They ate lots of weird food and talked mainly in **LATIN** and **ROMAN NUMERALS**

COGITO SUM AD NAUSEAM VXII

but after a long time they got fed up with all the **RUBBISH WEATHER** and the shortage of fresh **GARLIC** so they took all their **FINE WINE** and **SPAGHETTI** and they packed their bags and went back to warm and sunny **ROME**...

Byeeee!

ROME

... and what they left behind was the

DARK AGES

which were dark and muddy and also a bit **BORING** and it's in this time that I live, in a tiny village right down in the bottom left hand corner of **BRITAIN** where there's totally **NOTHING** to do and we live in **HOVELS** that are made from STRAW →  and **MUD**

We are all ~~extreemly~~ very **POOR** and we eat mostly **TURNIPS**

It rains a **LOT**

We mostly wear **TUNICS** that are **ROUGH** and **ITCHY** and they come in a variety of colours. Light brown, dark brown, mid brown, earth brown, mouse brown and brown. Everyone has loads of

Nits
Fleas →
Tangly hair
Mud
Bad Teeth
Zits

But in spite of **ALL** these things we are mostly **HAPPY**.

My friends
Eg ↓
Verucca
Dewzel my **PIG** ↓
Me (Sedric) ↓
Robin ↓
Urk ↓

(you have to turn over this page now...)

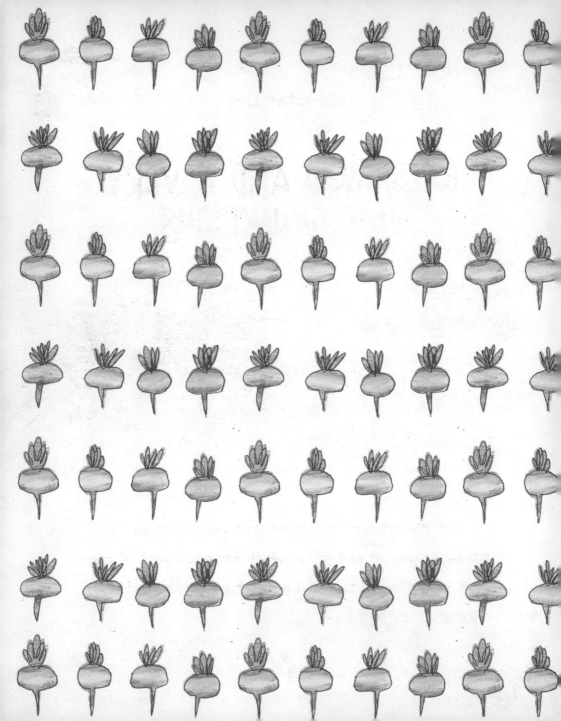

Chapter One

RATS, MUD AND A VERY RUDE AWAKENING

AAARRGH!

I woke up. Something horrible had landed on my face.

It was a rat.

And the rat was attached to a big lump of wet straw. A lump of wet straw which had been part of our roof until the rat munched a great big hole and fell through it on to me.

I was out of bed faster than a Roman with his toga on fire.

It wasn't a good start to the day, but it wasn't especially unusual because the rats in our village LOVE eating wet straw, which is what some idiot decided we should make our roofs from.

My mum started screaming and banging about with a broom and going completely bonkers because she's totally TERRIFIED of rats.

There are rats pretty much everywhere in our village so she screams pretty much all the time. Then she went even more bonkers with the broom because the rat was having a stress attack because it couldn't find the door, and then Denzel joined in which made Mum scream even LOUDER.

Denzel's my pig. He's very clever and funny, but my mum doesn't think so. She says he's a total pain who should live in the pigsty.

Just as Mum was getting to the completely screamingly insane stage, Verucca arrived. Verucca's my best friend. She's totally brilliant in a crisis.

'Hang on, Sedric's mum! I'll get it out for you!' she shouted.

Verucca's not at all scared of rats. In fact, she's not scared of **ANYTHING**. Except earwigs. She really hates earwigs. Someone told her

Earwig →

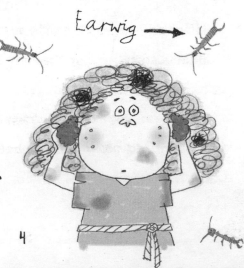

4

once that earwigs crawl into your ears and eat your brains when you're asleep, so she stuffs mud in her ears every night when she goes to bed so they can't get in. But I don't think earwigs REALLY do that. Eat your brains, I mean.

'Thank you, Verucca, love!' my mum shouted from the table that she'd climbed on to get away from the rat. 'Those blasted great things! We'll all be eaten in our beds one day – and then where will we be?'

Probably dead with bits missing, I thought.

Verucca picked up the rat by the tail and threw it out of the door.

Mum had just calmed down and made a cup of turnip tea when Dad came in. He'd been in the turnip field collecting turnips.

We grow a lot of turnips in our village. Actually turnips are pretty much all we grow which is fine if you like turnips (which I do) but pretty rubbish if you don't.

Mum told him about the rat.

'Well, rats is rats, Ethel, and there's nothing we can do about it,' said Dad.

He's full of pointless statements like that. Like when I suggest we make our hovel roofs from something that rats don't eat, he says, 'My father made his roof from straw and his father before him and his father before that. If it was good enough for them it's good enough for me.'

See what I mean?

Chapter Two

SOME STUFF ABOUT MY VILLAGE

Rubbish weather

By the time my mum had finished her turnip tea, it was time for Verucca and me to go to school.

We always go the long way round. We'd pretty much rather do **ANYTHING** than go to school, where we learn random stuff like reading and writing and sums and things about the Romans who used to live here but who went back to Rome when they got fed up with all the rubbish weather.

My dad says we're very lucky to have a school in our village as most villages don't have one.

They can have ours. I really wouldn't mind.

On the way to school Denzel did his 'running between our legs trying to trip us up' walk. This is funny but a bit annoying at the same time.

Verucca said, 'I had a weird dream last night, Sedric. Do you want to hear it?'

I didn't really want to, but I didn't want to hurt

her feelings either. The thing about other people's dreams is that they're really not that interesting because they're all inside someone else's head.

Verucca is always having weird dreams. She reckons she might be a witch when she grows up.

The only witch I know is Mad Warty Edna, who lives in a cave on the edge of the Dark Forest with a couple of toads. She's well skanky, with one tooth in the middle of her face.

MAD WARTY EDNA

Well skanky

One tooth

Toad

Verucca has round rosy cheeks and a mop of curly red hair so I think she's got a long way to go if she wants to be a witch. Unless she wants to be a sort of undercover witch who goes around looking like everyone else. Then she'd be fine.

So I sort of zoned out and just heard the bit at the end.

VERUCCA

Red curly hair

Round rosy cheeks

'. . . and then after this **HUGE** explosion we all fell down a big hole into some water and you – (although it wasn't **ACTUALLY** you but sort of a mixture of lots of people) – you started running around with a weird sort of dwarf dressed as a soldier and there was loads of shouting . . . and then we all had a big huge dinner with loads of strange food and this fat man shouted at everyone and then he exploded.'

You see what I mean about other people's dreams. They really don't make any sense.

Even taking the long way round, the walk to school is quite short. Our village is called Little Soggy-in-the-Mud and it's **VERY** small.

There are:

1. Some hovels. I'm not sure how many. I did start counting them once. There are definitely more than three. They are made mainly from mud and straw and they leak a lot.

2. A school, which is a slightly bigger hovel. It leaks a lot too.

3. A pigsty. Which hardly ever has pigs in it. It's mostly used for

HOVELS

School

Pigsty

visitors who don't mind the smell. (Denzel refuses to sleep in it although I tell my Mum he does. He actually sleeps in my bed.)

Turnip store

4. The turnip store. It's where we store all our turnips so we don't go hungry in the winter.

On the edge of our village is the Dark Forest which is huge and dark. No one likes going in there as it's full of goblins and trolls and dragons and bloodthirsty outlaws and weird scary monsters with bulging eyes.

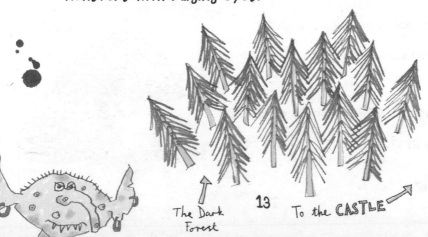

The Dark Forest

To the CASTLE

It's not really full of all those things. Grown-ups just tell us that stuff to keep us out. But there ARE actually outlaws. I know that because my friend Robin's cousin is one.

In the middle of the village is the Old Oak Tree. My dad says it was there when the Romans arrived which was before even HE was born and he's pretty ancient. We use it for all sorts of things. The grown-ups have meetings under it to talk about Important Stuff and to drink turnip cider and we stick up notices and posters on it, like this one:

Littel Soggy-in-the-Mud

VILLIJ FARE

Splat the rat wiv REEL rats

Yummy Turnip based fud

xtra STRONG SID A

Lots of Sider

On the other side of the village is a big hill with a castle on the top.

It's the usual sort of castle. Big and stony with battlements and turrets and those little slitty windows for firing arrows through.

The baron who lived in the castle was called Baron Osric the Incredibly Old. He was really nice, and he didn't bother us much, apart from coming down once a year to open our village fair and sending us stuff at Christmas.

So that's it. Little Soggy-in-the-Mud. It's not very exciting, what with there being nothing to do and it raining absolutely ALL the time and mud absolutely EVERYWHERE and nothing to eat but turnips, but it's my village and I quite liked it just the way it was, and I really thought it was going to stay the same forever.

But it didn't.

Chapter Three

A BIT ABOUT SCHOOL AND SOME SHOUTING

When Verucca, Denzel and I reached the school,
everyone was hanging about outside waiting for Gaius,
our teacher, to arrive. My other best friends Eg,
Urk and Robin were already there playing Sticks and
Stones. It's our favourite game and here's how you
play it:

Each player has a stick and a stone.

Player 1 hits their stone into the mud with their stick.

They keep hitting the stone until it sinks into the mud.

Player 2 then has their turn while Player 1 looks for their stone.

The game is won when neither player can be bothered to look for any more stones.

I'd just found a really good stick when Gaius arrived.

Gaius is Roman and he's massively old and wrinkly. He's the only Roman left for miles around. He didn't go back to Rome when all the other Romans left. He says he likes living here. He likes the way the British talk about the weather all the time and the hot sun in Rome used to make him come out in a rash AND he's

Gaius

Breakfast

allergic to garlic. I think he's a bit bonkers. I mean, who wouldn't rather go to Rome where it's lovely and sunny and warm instead of staying here in all the rain and the cold and the mud?

Gaius may be bonkers but he's really, really clever too. He's read loads of books AND he speaks Latin. He often forgets what he's saying in the middle of saying it though and he sometimes falls asleep randomly

in the middle of a lesson because he's so massively old, and you can tell what he's had for breakfast because there is always bits of it down the front of his toga.

There's usually a lot of pushing and shoving when we go into school because everyone wants to sit at the back. Verucca's brilliant at pushing because she's the biggest so she saves me a seat next to her. Denzel isn't allowed in school, but he sometimes gets in when Gaius isn't looking and hides under my chair.

← School

This morning Gaius must have seen his little curly tail sticking out or something because he said, 'I believe there is a pig under your seat, Sedric. You know the rules. No pigs in class.'

So Denzel got up and trotted outside while Gaius got out the register.

'Verucca?'

'Here, sir.'

'Eg?'

'Here, sir.'

'Sedric?'

'Here, sir.'

'Urk?'

Gaius looked up at Urk and frowned, then he peered at him really closely. Urk's well ugly, with loads of zits and hair like spiky fungus. His hair's always full of gigantic nits so his mum cuts it really short – but the nits still hang on so it doesn't make any difference. He reckons it's because his head tastes better than ours do. Haha!

Anyway, Gaius was staring at Urk, so we all crowded round too. He had weird black things stuck to his face.

'You appear to have something stuck to your face, Urk,' said Gaius.

'It's slugs,' said Urk.

'And may I ask why you have slugs stuck to your

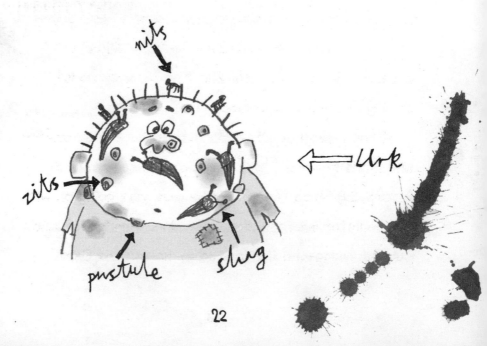

nits

zits

Urk

pustule

slug

22

face?' said Gaius.

SLUG →

'It was Eg's idea, sir,' said Urk. 'He told me if I put slugs on my zits that they'd disappear.'

'Is this true, Eg? Did you tell Urk that if he put slugs on his zits they would disappear?' We all sniggered. It was the way Gaius said 'zits', like it was foreign or something.

'Well, Mad Warty Edna said it would work,' said Eg. Everyone knows Mad Warty Edna is ACTUALLY as mad as a bucket of weasels, but Eg will believe anything. He was the one who told Verucca about earwigs eating your brains.

'May I suggest you don't take advice from anyone who has the word MAD in front of their name in future, Eg,' said Gaius, and he was just going on with the register when suddenly the door burst open and Rubella swaggered in followed by her friend Gert.

Gert is short with loads of zits and
she never says anything, and
Rubella complains about
absolutely everything.

'OMIGOD! Why
do I even have to be
here? School's just
POINTLESS and
BORING and we
never learn anything
useful except just
total RUBBISH and
stuff!'

'Could you please sit down, Rubella, dear. I would
like to start the lesson,' said Gaius.

Rubella walked as slowly as she could to a seat
and flopped down, sighing. Unfortunately it was the
one next to Urk, and when she saw his face she went

off on one again. 'What is that stuck to his face, sir? That is SOOO gross. I shouldn't have to sit next to THAT, should I? Honestly this village is just totally RUBBISH! It's all just MUD and TURNIPS and people with DISGUSTING things stuck to their faces!'

Gaius ignored her and got on with calling the register.

'Robin? Hood down, please,' said Gaius. 'You know the rules about wearing hoodies in class.'

'It's so unfair, sir. It's my right as a human being to express my individuality through my clothes.'

'Rules are rules, young Robin, and they are there to be obeyed!'

Gaius always says that, but he never says who makes up the rules in the first place.

We started with Roman history (as usual), and Gaius had just launched into some story about a battle between the Romans and the Picks and the Snots or something, when we heard shouting coming from outside.

SNOTS

ROMANS

PICKS

26

There are a few reasons why there might be shouting in our village:

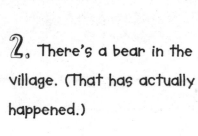

1. It's my mum and she's found a rat.

2. There's a bear in the village. (That has actually happened.)

3. Eg's grandad has discovered that someone has moved his conker collection.

4. It's Sergeant Hengist.

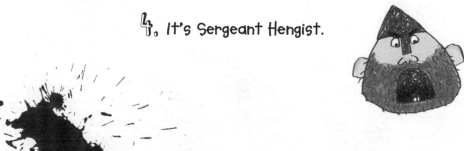

Chapter Four

MORE SHOUTING AND SOME SERIOUSLY NOT VERY GOOD NEWS

It was Sergeant Hengist.

He's the sergeant in charge of the castle and he shouts pretty much ALL the time. I reckon he's louder than my mum and that's saying something.

So we all charged outside to see what was going on. Denzel was well pleased to see me and jumped about wagging his little tail.

Sergeant Hengist and some soldiers were marching into the village, but the soldiers weren't

doing very well with the
marching thing on account
of all the mud. They kept
on getting stuck.

'LEFT-RIGHT,
LEFT-RIGHT!
PICK THOSE
FEET UP, YOU

'ORRIBLE LOT! CALL YOURSELVES SOLDIERS? MY DEAR OLD WHITE-HAIRED MOTHER COULD DO BETTER THAN THAT!'

shouted the sergeant.

One of the soldiers said, 'Sarge. This marching thing's a bit tricky what with it being all muddy and everything. Couldn't we just sort of walk?'

'Yeah, sarge,' said another one. 'My boots are all wet and they're rubbing something 'orrible.'

The sergeant said that maybe they would like to work in the castle kitchens washing up instead as they were obviously both such GIRLS!

'How DARE he!' hissed Verucca. 'What's wrong with girls?'

The soldiers squelched towards us and slithered to a stop. Sergeant Hengist stuck out his huge chain mail chest and narrowed his one good eye. The other one doesn't work very well so you're never quite sure which eye is looking at you, which is a bit confusing.

'VILLAGERS OF LITTLE SOGGY-IN-THE-MUD,' he boomed. 'I HAVE AN ANNOUNCEMENT TO MAKE!'

There was a lot of muttering from the grown-ups. Stuff like, 'Ooh. An announcement. I love an announcement, don't you?' and then, 'Oh yes, I know what you mean. Announcements always cheer me up.'

What is it with grown-ups? They sometimes talk such a load of rubbish. I think that one day they must get a birthday card with a certificate that says:

I just hope I never get one when I'm grown up.

Sergeant Hengist was losing patience.

'WILL YOU ALL JUST SHUT UP AND LISTEN!'

A blob of spit flew out of his mouth as he shouted and it hit Urk, who was standing right in front of him.

'Charming!' said Verucca loudly. She wiped the spit off Urk, who didn't seem to have noticed.

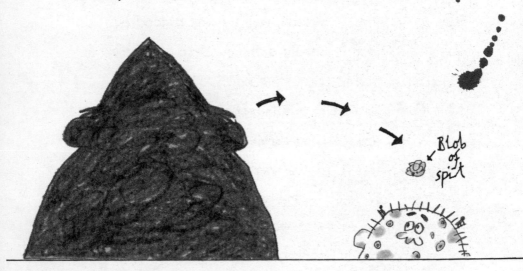

Blob of spit

'I HAVE COME HERE TODAY,' continued the sergeant, 'TO TELL YOU THAT BARON OSRIC THE INCREDIBLY OLD IS DEAD AND THAT HIS NEPHEW, BARON DENNIS, HAS TAKEN OVER THE CASTLE!'

There were a few gasps of surprise as everyone took in the news and then more randomly stupid murmurings, like, 'Oh dear, well he was a good age wasn't he?' and, 'There's a thing, who'd have thought it?'

I must admit I was a bit gutted. I'd never known a time when Osric the Incredibly Old hadn't been in the castle. But I suppose his name should have given me a hint that he couldn't have gone on forever.

But the sergeant hadn't finished.

'BARON DENNIS WANTS YOU ALL TO KNOW THAT THERE ARE GOING TO BE SOME BIG CHANGES AROUND HERE, DUE TO THE FACT THAT HIS UNCLE, BARON OSRIC THE INCREDIBLY OLD, HAS LET THE CASTLE GO TO RACK AND RUIN, WITH DRY ROT AND

WOODWORM AND OTHER BAD
STUFF!' He paused to glare at us before going on.
'SO FROM NOW ON, EVERY FAMILY
IN THE VILLAGE
IS GOING TO
HAVE TO PAY
ENORMOUS
TAXES!'

Woodworms
(eating wood)

'What did he say?' said Eg's grandad.

'He said Baron Dennis has got dry rot,' my mum
shouted in his ear.

'Why's he telling us that?' said Eg's grandad. 'We
can't do anything about it.'

'What are these enormous taxes he wants us to
pay anyway?' my dad asked the sergeant.

'The baron wants your money to pay for repairs to
the castle!' said Sergeant Hengist crossly.

36

'Money?' said Verucca's mum, Mildred. 'We haven't got any money!'

That was actually true. I'd never even SEEN any money. Not in my whole life.

'What, none of you?' said the sergeant, glaring at us with his one good eye as if he was expecting someone to suddenly put up their hand and say, *Actually I've got loads of money! How much do you want?* 'Well, what HAVE you got, then?' he asked.

'Turnips,' said my dad.

Chapter Five

A BIT OF SPYING

So Sergeant Hengist ordered everyone to hand over their turnips.

The soldiers couldn't carry many. They'd only brought tiny bags to put the money in so they said they'd have to come back later with bigger bags.

I expected all the grown-ups to be really angry or SOMETHING, because without our turnips we'd have totally nothing to eat, but they didn't do anything. They all just wandered off looking miserable.

Robin got quite excited and said that we should run away and live in the Dark Forest as outlaws. Verucca told him to stop being silly and as the grown-ups weren't going to do anything, it was down to us to think of a plan to stop the baron. So we all thought for a while and we finally came up with four choices which were:

1. We could kill the new baron. (This was Robin's idea and was generally thought to be a Bad Idea for lots of reasons. Mainly because killing people is a bit wrong and we'd most probably be arrested and hanged.)

2. We could hide the rest of the turnips somewhere else **REALLY** quickly so when the soldiers came back for more, they couldn't find them. (This was a slightly better idea but still not brilliant.)

3. We could follow the soldiers up to the castle to do some spying and check out this new baron and see what was really going on. This seemed to be a Good Idea as it also meant we didn't have to go back to school.

4. And I forgot what number four was.

PLANS to stop the BARON

No. 1 kill him

No. 2 Hide turnips

No. 3 Do some spying

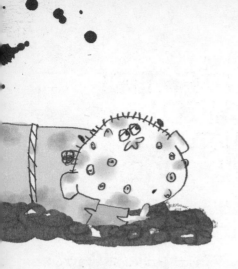

So Verucca, Eg, Urk, Robin, Denzel and I followed the soldiers up to the castle.

We kept a safe distance behind. Robin said we should be in Stealth Mode, which meant we had to keep jumping behind bushes and zigzagging across the hill like rabbits. Denzel didn't get the hang of Stealth Mode so we fell over him a lot.

As we got closer to the castle we heard a lot of people shouting stuff, like:

'DON'T DROP THAT YOU IDIOT IT'S VERY VALUABLE!'

and 'YOU TAKE THE OTHER END!
I'LL PUSH IT FROM HERE!' and
'COULD YOU GET THAT OFF MY
FOOT PLEASE BECAUSE I THINK
MY TOE'S BROKEN!'

It all sounded very strange and mysterious, so
we hid behind a prickly bush to see what was going on.

prickly
bush

Chapter Six

WE DISCOVER SOME VERY IMPORTANT STUFF

In front of the castle were loads of carts piled high with the strangest stuff I've ever seen in my life.

Soldiers were unloading it and carrying it into the castle. It all looked like it cost an AWFUL lot of money.

I peered through the bush and said, 'WOW, look at this!' and Robin said, 'What? I can't see.' There was a scuffling noise behind me and Eg said, 'OW!' very loudly and Verucca said, 'Shush, they'll hear us!' and Eg said,

'I've really, really hurt myself!'

'What's going on here?' said Eg as he squeezed through next to me. His face was all scratched and bleeding.

'It looks as if the stuff about the castle falling down was all big fat lies,' whispered Verucca. 'The baron wants our taxes to pay for all this posh new furniture and stuff!'

'Will you look at that!' said Urk, who'd pushed himself through the prickles behind Eg.

He was pointing at some soldiers who were carrying a big naked lady. Well, not a REAL naked lady.

That would have been gross. This one was made out of stone. She was COMPLETELY naked except for a bit of floaty stuff covering her bits and pieces.

Urk and Eg did some sniggering. Urk said he could see her bum.

'WATCH WHAT YOU'RE DOING WITH THAT STATUE YOU IDIOTS! IT'S EXTREMELY VALUABLE!' The voice came from a fat man in a purple toga who was coming out of the castle.

'Who is THAT?' hissed Verucca.

'I think it might be the new baron,' I whispered.

'He looks like a greedy fat toad to me,' said

Robin darkly.

Sergeant Hengist came out of the castle.

'Well, sergeant. Any news?'

said the new baron.

'I made the announcement to the

peasants, sire, as you requested,'

said the sergeant.

'And?'

'And what, sire?'

'Did you get the taxes?'

'Er, not exactly, sire.'

'What do you mean **NOT EXACTLY?**
What **DID** you get?' the baron said.

'Turnips, sire,' said Sergeant Hengist,

looking at his feet.

Turnips

'TURNIPS? WHAT DO
YOU MEAN, TURNIPS?'

'Well they didn't have any actual money, sire. They only had turnips.'

The baron's eyes went all goggly. It made him look even more like a toad. One that's been squeezed REALLY hard. (Not that I have EVER squeezed a toad. Well, I did once, but that was an accident.)

Another turnip

Sergeant Hengist was sweating a bit and running his finger round the collar of his chainmail like he couldn't breathe very well.

'TURNIPS!' said the baron again. 'What exactly am I supposed to do with

TURNIPS? TURNIPS won't buy anything! They won't buy incredibly expensive furniture ordered by my wife and shipped at great expense from ROME! What earthly good are TURNIPS? You can't even EAT them!'

'The peasants do actually eat them, sire. In fact I think turnips are all they eat,' said Sergeant Hengist.

turnips →

'Good grief, do they?' said the baron. 'So how many turnips have these stinking peasants got?'

'They've got quite a lot, sire,' said the sergeant.

'So would these turnips fetch a lot of cash at market, then?' said the baron, rubbing his hands.

'I should think so, sire,' said the sergeant.

Just then a fat woman in a pink toga came out of the castle. 'Dennis!' she shouted. 'Gluteus has almost finished but he says he needs some more gold to

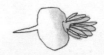

pay for the marble he's ordered from Rome.'

'But I can't afford it, Prunehilda, my sweet,' said the baron. 'Why can't he use wood? We've got plenty of wood. Wood doesn't cost anything – the forest's full of it!'

'Oh don't be silly, Dennis!' squawked Prunehilda. 'Gluteus darling, come and tell my husband why we simply MUST have the marble!'

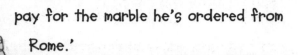

A man carrying a hammer and some metal tubes joined them. He was wearing a toga too. What was it with all this toga-wearing stuff? Had everyone gone

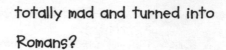

totally mad and turned into Romans?

'Salve, sire,' said the man in the toga, bowing low. 'The trendimus at the moment in Rome is absolutelio in vino veritas the marble.'

'Ooh! Listen to that, Dennis!' said Prunehilda. 'That's PROPER Latin that is!'

'Pro bono ad infinitum, my lady,' said the Roman, winking and smiling an oily smile at Prunehilda.

'Oh Gluteus! You are naughty!' she giggled. 'Dennis – he said we really MUST have the marble!'

'Did he, my sweet?' said Dennis wearily.

'That's not PROPER Latin,' whispered Verucca angrily. 'He's talking complete RUBBISH!'

The baron turned to Sergeant Hengist, who was standing waiting nervously. 'Well, sergeant. You heard her ladyship! I'll be needing a lot more turnips if I'm going to pay for marble from Rome as well as all THIS . . .' and he waved his hand at the cartloads of Roman stuff, 'so you need to get back down to the village and get some.'

'Yes, sire,' said the sergeant.

'In fact, as soon as I've had my lunch I think I'll come down to the village with you. This might be a very good opportunity to introduce myself to these peasants.'

As the baron went back into the castle talking to himself, I had a think about all the stuff we'd found out from our spying exercise:

1. The baron didn't need our turnips to pay for the castle repairs at all and he was therefore a BIG FAT LIAR!

2. He was also stupid and thought the idiot in the toga talking rubbish Latin was a real Roman.

3. Sergeant Hengist was scared of him (VERY important).

Shedloads of turnips →

Chapter Seven

SOME VERY USEFUL NEW FRIENDS

'What are we going to do, Rog? He'll go completely BONKERS when he finds out.'

'Hang on, Norm. I'll think of something.'

'Thought of anything yet?'

'No.'

We'd gone a little way down the hill when we saw Roger and Norman, the two soldiers who'd complained about the marching thing earlier, looking down at the broken remains of quite a big Roman pot.

I asked them what the matter was, mostly out of politeness. It didn't take a genius to work out

what had happened.

'It just slipped out of my hands,' said Roger. 'The baron's going to kill us when he finds out.'

'Well don't show him then,' said Verucca.

'What?'

'Hide the evidence,' I said.

'I think they might have something there, Rog,' said Norman.

Roger looked puzzled. 'What. Not tell the baron?'

'Exactly,' I said. I knew what I was talking about. Whenever I break anything in our hovel I dig a hole and bury it. Mum just thinks she's lost it or something. Mind you, if she ever starts digging by the pigsty just to the right of the Old Oak Tree I'll be in SERIOUS trouble.

Archaeologist (quite a few hundred years later)

broken pot

BIG HOLE

So we helped them dig a big hole.

Denzel joined in for a bit but he lost interest when he couldn't find any acorns.

'So what's it like in the castle with the new baron, then?' I asked as we filled in the hole. I'm really good at finding out stuff using STEALTH. The secret is to pretend you're not really all that interested.

'Oh, don't get me started,' said Roger. 'If he's not getting us to carry stuff all over the place it's "Do this, do that!" from his wife all day long. We're soldiers, I keep on saying, don't I Norm? Not flaming removal men. And we're doing all sorts of stupid stuff that wasn't in our job description.'

'Oh?' I said. 'Like what?'

'Well,' said Norman, 'me and Rog have been carrying metal pipes and wood and stuff

all the way up to the Great Bathroom,
like servants!'

'If you ask me, it's her
what really wants this
Great Big Bubbly Bath
Thingy what they're building. I don't
think he's all that keen.'

I thought this sounded interesting, so I said,
'What's this Great Big Bubbly Bath Thingy?'

'Well,' said Roger. 'There's this bloke, right. Calls

himself Gluteus Maximus or some stupid name, wears a toga. He's building this thing and he says he's a genuine Roman plumber, but my wife's sister's neighbour knows him and she says he's not a REAL Roman at all. He's called Dave and he comes from Essex.'

So THAT'S who the bloke was who was talking all that rubbish Latin, I thought.

'I thought it was strange when I asked him how he'd got here,' said Norman. 'He said he came by horse and cart. Well I know for a fact that to get here from Rome you have to cross at least one sea and you can't do that in a horse and cart. Well, you could . . . but you'd drown.'

'Norm, we'd better get a move on,' said Roger anxiously, 'before SHE starts yelling again.'

So we said goodbye and they headed back to the castle.

I was feeling pretty pleased with myself.

How to get from ROME to our village

Picks live here

Snots live here

LITTLE SOGGY-IN-THE-MUD

SEA very wet and definitely not to be attempted without a boat.

ROME

We had made two **VERY** useful friends and found out loads of stuff about the new baron. Stuff like:

1. There was something very big and expensive being built in the castle. (Still not totally sure what though.)

2. Roger and Norman were definitely not happy with the new baron or his wife.

3. Gluteus Maximus wasn't just not a proper Roman, his name wasn't even a proper name. Verucca said it was Latin for Big Bum.

Urk and Eg sniggered a lot at that. Anything with the word 'bum' in it makes them laugh.

As we headed back down to the village it started to rain. It was just a few big drops at first. Then

Us going downhill

there were more and more until by
the time we got to the village water
was running in streams down the hill.

Gaius was in the middle of a handwriting lesson
when we got back to school. He asked us where we'd
been, so we told him all about what we'd seen up at
the castle, and about Roger and Norman and the Great

Big Bubbly Bath Thingy. Urk asked Gaius what a bath was and Gaius said it was a sort of huge giant barrel filled with hot water that the Romans loved sitting in for hours with no clothes on. It sounded well boring and pointless.

'The new baron doesn't want our turnips for repairs to the castle at all, does he, sir?' said Robin. 'He's just taking advantage of us peasants because he's a greedy fat toad, isn't he?'

'I'm very much afraid that you are right, young Robin, and sadly there is little any of us can do. As baron he owns our village and all of you and the land for miles around. He is very powerful.'

'There must be SOMETHING we can do, sir,' I said. 'Osric would never have taken our turnips, would he?'

'No, he certainly wouldn't, young Sedric. In fact I have a vague recollection that he was planning to leave

A LITTLE KNOWN FACT ABOUT THE ROMANS

and how they got beaten.

Salve sires! The barbarians are attacking!

The Romans loved having baths SO much that they stopped doing conquering so they got all pink and fat.

Barbarian

a small bequest to the village in his will.'

Urk asked what a bequest was and Gaius said it was like a sort of present, and a will was a list of stuff that you give to your friends when you die.

If I died my list would be very short.

I would leave Denzel to Verucca.

There wouldn't be much else. Except my dried toad and my stone shaped like a skull. I don't think anyone would get very excited about my will.

But Osric's will. Now that was a completely different thing.

Chapter Eight

MUD AND A
SUDDEN VISIT

Gaius said we'd talked enough about baths and wills and that we needed to do some more handwriting. We didn't do much though because he fell asleep so the whole class went outside.

It wasn't raining so much now, and it was very muddy.

We have different levels of mud in our village:

LEVEL 1 - A bit sticky but mostly OK.

LEVEL 2 – Very squelchy. Not good for anything with wheels.

LEVEL 3 – Dangerous to tiny children and small animals.

Today's mud was Level 3, so we played Sticks and Stones but with bigger stones.

Robin got a bit over-excited and accidently hit Eg on the nose with his stone which made his nose bleed.

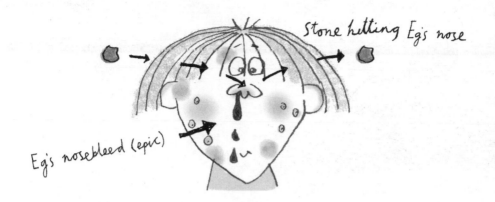

Stone hitting Eg's nose

Eg's nosebleed (epic)

Eg has epic nosebleeds. They can go on for hours. He often uses them to get out of lessons or to scare old ladies.

We'd just started to get a bit bored with Sticks and Stones and Eg's nosebleed when we heard a noise like a duck being strangled. Verucca said it wasn't a duck, it was a trumpet, and it was coming from the castle.

We looked up the hill and we could see a strange sort of procession. Some soldiers were pulling something large down from the castle towards the village. As they got nearer, the procession started to speed up.

'HENGIST! WHY ARE WE GOING SO FAST?' shouted someone who sounded like the baron.

'The chariot won't stop, sire!'

'WHAT DO YOU MEAN IT WON'T STOP? GET YOUR IDIOT SOLDIERS TO SLOW DOWN OR WE'LL CRASH!'

There was a high-pitched squawk that sounded like a rusty wheel, but the soldiers and the thing they were pulling just carried on getting faster and faster until they all reached the mud at the bottom of the hill and sank.

'What is THAT?' said Eg. We all crept nearer to get a closer look.

'That' was a huge shiny golden cart thing painted all over with pictures and covered in curly bits and jewels. Standing up in the back of it clutching the sides were the baron and his wife. They looked WELL sick which was most probably from being bounced around a lot on the way down.

Eg tried to touch it. He loves to fiddle with things. He usually fiddles too much and then he breaks stuff.

Bad smell

'Hengist!' hissed Prunehilda through gritted teeth. 'Why have we stopped, and what's that DISGUSTING smell?'

'The chariot's stuck in the mud, your ladyship, and it's the peasants.'

'What?' said Urk. 'We don't smell.'

So I said that we did actually. Well, he did. But not in a bad way.

'That is SO the most gorgeous thing that I've ever seen in my whole entire LIFE! What is it?' whispered Rubella.

'It's a Roman chariot,' said Verucca.

'I knew that,' I said. (I didn't really.)

'No you didn't,' said Verucca.

'How DO you know this stuff?' Eg asked Verucca, stroking the chariot wheels.

'I listen,' she said, pulling Eg away from the chariot. Verucca can be SO annoying sometimes.

'Are we going to stand here in the rain forever in this putrid cesspit of a village, Dennis, or are you going to get your useless soldiers to PULL US OUT?' complained Prunehilda.

'Of course not, my sweet – we'll be out of here in no time,' said Dennis.

'HENGIST! WILL YOU GET YOUR USELESS SOLDIERS TO PULL US OUT OF THIS MUD!'

The soldiers did their best. They pulled and they
pushed and they grunted and sweated. But the chariot
wouldn't move.

'I think that maybe his lordship and his wife are a
bit too – er – heavy, sarge,' whispered Roger. 'We'll
never shift it with them standing on the back.'

'ARE YOU CALLING ME FAT?'

boomed the baron. He had very sharp ears. My mum says I have sharp ears. That doesn't mean that they're all pointy – it just means that I hear things she doesn't want me to.

'No, sire, of course not, sire,' said Roger.

'Good. Where are these blasted peasants anyway, Hengist? Why haven't they come out to greet me?'

'I don't think they knew you were coming, sire,' said the sergeant looking weary. 'They're over there sheltering from the rain.' And he pointed to where my mum and dad and the rest of the villagers were standing underneath the Old Oak Tree.

Chapter Nine

A LOT MORE MUD AND SOME VERY BIG LIES

'If you could get down and walk over to speak to them, sire, then we could get this over with and we could all get back to the castle,' said Sergeant Hengist nervously. The rain was getting heavier.

'WALK? IN THIS MUD? DO YOU HAVE ANY IDEA WHAT THESE SHOES COST?'

Sergeant Hengist said he didn't. I didn't either. I didn't even know you could actually BUY shoes. We don't usually wear anything on our feet. When it gets cold in the winter we just tie sacks round them with bits of string.

Sacks   String   Peasant's legs

'So walking's out of the question then, sire?'

'Yes it most certainly is,' said the baron.

'Dennis,' hissed Prunehilda, 'if you don't hurry up and do whatever you came to do and get me out of this rain-drenched mud-soaked stinking sewer of a village I am going to have to start screaming . . .'

'Got any other suggestions, Hengist?' said the baron.

'You could shout, sire,' said the sergeant.

'Will they hear me?' said the baron.

'I doubt it, sire, but it's worth a try,' he said.

'VILLAGERS OF LITTLE SOGGY-IN-THE-MUD...' began the baron. 'I HAVE COME HERE TODAY TO INTRODUCE MYSELF AND MY LOVELY WIFE PRUNEHILDA...'

'What did he say?' shouted Eg's grandad from under the Old Oak Tree.

'He said he's got a lovely wife,' shouted Mildred.

'Why would he tell us that?' shouted Eg's grandad. 'Does he think we're interested?'

The baron carried on. '. . .

AND TO OFFER YOU THE OPPORTUNITY OF A LIFETIME!'

'Speak up, we can't hear you!' shouted Mildred.

'IN ORDER TO REPAIR OUR LOVELY CASTLE I NEED TO TAKE ALL YOUR TURNIPS, BUT IN RETURN YOU WILL HAVE THE GRATITUDE OF MY WIFE AND

MYSELF, AND THE SATISFACTION OF KNOWING THAT WITHOUT YOUR HELP OUR MAGNIFICENT CASTLE WOULD HAVE FALLEN DOWN.'

'What's he going on about now?' shouted Eg's grandad.

'He says he's taking all our turnips to stop his castle falling down,' shouted my mum.

'That's nice,' said Mildred.

I couldn't stand any more.

'DON'T LISTEN TO HIM!' I shouted. 'THE CASTLE'S NOT FALLING DOWN! HE WANTS OUR TURNIPS SO HE CAN PAY FOR ALL HIS EXPENSIVE ROMAN STUFF. BUT WE NEED THEM OR WE'RE ALL GOING TO STARVE!'

The baron turned and glared at me, then he quickly

80

forced a smile. It was the tight smile of someone who doesn't smile very often. 'Now who put that idea into your silly little head? OF COURSE the turnips are for repairs to the castle.'

'NO THEY'RE NOT!' shouted Verucca. 'IT'S LIKE SEDRIC SAID. THEY'RE TO PAY FOR ALL YOUR FANCY STATUES AND FURNITURE AND STUFF!'

The baron's smile froze. 'Hengist!' he hissed under his breath. 'Get rid of them! And if they cause any trouble throw them in the dungeons with the rats!'

I didn't like the sound of that, but before the sergeant could do anything, Prunehilda started screaming and flapping her arms. A swarm of angry wasps were buzzing around her head.

I looked around to see where they were coming from and spotted a small hooded figure crouching over a

tree stump by the
bridge.

It was Robin.
He was poking a
stick into a hole in
the tree and clouds of
wasps were pouring out and
heading towards us.

Oh dear, I thought. This is going
to end VERY badly.

This one is specially cross

Angry wasps ↓

Chapter Ten

WASPS!

There was a lot of shouting and flapping of arms.
The wasps were very angry and so was the baron.
Prunehilda just screamed and screamed and when
she wasn't screaming she was having a go at Dennis
about how she was never EVER coming back to our
disgusting village as long as she lived. Which was fine
by me. We didn't ask her to come in the first place. I
was hoping that while her mouth was open a wasp might
fly in. THAT would have shut her up.

The soldiers were still trying to pull the chariot out
of the mud but it was just sinking deeper.

'HENGIST!' yelled the baron. 'WHERE
IN HADES ARE YOU? WHY AREN'T

YOU GETTING US OUT OF HERE?!'

'OOWW! DENNIS!' screamed Prunehilda. 'I've been stung and there's a wasp in my HAIR! GET IT OUT NOW!'

Prunehilda flapped her arms in a panic but there wasn't much room in the back of the chariot and as she

flapped she hit Dennis, who lost his balance, and they
both fell backwards off the chariot into the Level 3 mud.

Just at that moment Denzel got a tiny bit over-
excited, and before I could stop him he jumped on top
of Prunehilda and ran around in circles wagging his little
tail and licking her face.

He really seemed to like her. Maybe she reminded
him of his mother. Prunehilda did look a bit like a pig.

Anyway, Prunehilda screamed and screamed a bit more and then she must have fainted because the screaming stopped. The baron didn't faint, though.

'HENGIST! Get us out of here now and ARREST THE PIG!' he shouted.

I thought I must have misheard him, but then Sergeant Hengist shouted at the soldiers, 'You heard what his lordship said –

ARREST THE PIG!'

'What are we arresting it for?' said one.

'FOR JUST BEING THERE! DO I HAVE TO EXPLAIN EVERYTHING?' shouted the baron. 'TAKE IT TO THE KITCHENS AND GIVE IT TO THE COOK! And Hengist, get the cart and collect

ALL the turnips in the village and if any of those stinking peasants object just tell them about the CONSEQUENCES!

Then there was an awful lot more shouting as Dennis and Prunehilda were pulled out of the mud. There were a LOT of rude words, but they were finally carried off, back up the hill to the castle.

Then a huge, scary-looking soldier picked up Denzel.

His little piggy eyes looked all sad and confused, and I could only watch as he was carried away.

It had all happened so quickly.

Why didn't I stop him jumping on Prunehilda?

Perhaps I should have trained him better. I was trying really hard not to cry and Verucca put her arm round me and gave me a hug, but Sergeant Hengist was still shouting. 'RIGHT, YOU HORRIBLE PEASANTS! MY SOLDIERS HERE ARE COMING ROUND WITH A CART. YOU'RE TO GIVE THEM ALL YOUR TURNIPS AND IF ANYONE REFUSES THERE WILL BE CONSEQUENCES!'

There was the usual mumbling of stupid stuff, like, 'What are consequences then?' and, 'Don't ask me,' and, 'Aren't they a bit like blackberries?' and, 'No – I think they're those things you dunk in turnip tea.'

'So what exactly ARE consequences?' shouted Verucca.

Sergeant Hengist pushed his hairy face right up close to Verucca's. 'Consequences means that if you don't give me all your turnips right now then BAD things will happen!'

'What sort of bad things?' said Verucca, looking him right in the eye.

'Hmm – let me think – oh yes. I know. Bad things like hovels catching fire, children disappearing and people being mysteriously poisoned. I'm sure you understand me.'

So consequences are just threats then, but harder to spell.

'RIGHT, MEN! GET THE CART LOADED!' shouted the sergeant.

'Cart? What cart, sarge?' said Norman.

The sergeant's one good eye narrowed again. The other one started to twitch.

'The cart you brought to collect the turnips in, STUPID!'

'But you never said anything about a cart, sarge. You just said to clean the chariot and get the baron and his wife down to the village.'

I watched the sergeant look around blankly as he realised Norman was right. He'd forgotten to bring a cart.

Have you ever noticed how when people are wrong it makes them angry with the person who points it out?

'Well, don't just stand there like an idiot.

Sergeant Hengist REALLY very cross indeed because he's realised he's forgotten to bring a cart.

FIND ONE!' shouted the sergeant.

'But where, sarge?' said Norman.

Our turnip cart was sticking out from behind the turnip store. The sergeant's beady eye spotted it.

'OVER THERE! TAKE THAT ONE! GOOD GRIEF, DO I HAVE TO THINK OF EVERYTHING?'

So we watched the soldiers load up **OUR** cart with all of **OUR** turnips. We would have none left.

No turnips at all. And no turnips meant we would all starve.

What WERE we going to do?

Chapter Eleven

PROTESTS
AND PLACARDS

My belly woke me up the next morning. It was gurgling and grumbling like a hollow log that's got rats gnawing away on the insides.

LOG ➝

I looked down and there was a small Denzel—shaped empty space at the end of my bed.

Rat gnawing

I felt more miserable than I can ever remember feeling before in my whole life.

I got out of bed. Mum put a plate in front of me with some green stuff on it.

'What's that?' I asked her.

'It's a lovely bit of grass, Sedric. Your dad cut it fresh this morning. It's quite nice once you get used to the horrible taste.'

I said thanks but I'd pass on the grass. I make a point of not eating anything GREEN. We grew some green stuff once. Little round things. They were DISGUSTING. I think they were called sprouts.

Sprouts (yuk)

Verucca arrived. My mum tried to get her to have some grass too but she said her mum had made her some boiled nettles for breakfast so she was fine, thank you.

'We will get Denzel back, Sedric, you know that,

don't you?' she said as we walked to school. 'Whatever we have to do, we WILL save him.'

'Thanks, Verucca,' I said. I so wanted to believe her, but I kept thinking about Denzel being served up on a plate to the fat baron and his fat wife. My mum sometimes used to threaten to cook him herself when he'd really annoyed her, like when he got over–excited once and knocked

over a whole pan

of turnip

soup she'd

been making,

or when she

tripped over him when

he was having a nap in

the middle of the floor

and she knocked one of

her teeth out.

She was well cross then and said all sorts of horrible things, but I knew she didn't mean them.

Prunehilda looked as though she'd most probably eat Denzel as a light snack though, judging by the size of her.

When we got to school Gaius was taking the register.

'Robin?'

'Yes, sir.'

'By the way, Robin,' Gaius said quietly, 'the wasp incident is NOT to be repeated.' Robin nodded and went pink. 'Fine,' said Gaius. 'We won't mention it again then. Urk?'

There was no answer.

'Has anybody seen young Urk?' asked Gaius.

We all shook our heads. Eg said he'd probably starved to death, which was what we were ALL going to do now the baron had taken all our turnips. Our bellies were making really loud rumbling noises that sounded like thunder.

RUMBLE

Us all starving

RUMBLE

Rumble

Just then Urk appeared in the doorway. He looked very pale. 'Sorry I'm late, sir, but I've been close to death.'

'Explain yourself, Urk,' said Gaius.

'Well, yesterday,' said Urk, 'after the baron took all our turnips, I was WELL hungry and Mad Warty Edna gave me some stuff she'd made out of some weird roots. It smelled horrible but she said it was all right

so I ate it anyway because I was STARVING only it turned out it wasn't all right and now I'm really tired because I haven't slept much what with the squits and throwing up and everything.'

'That is SO gross – tell him to shut up, sir,' said Rubella.

'A little too much information, Urk, but thank you for sharing,' said Gaius.

I was getting a bit fed up with all the stuff about Urk's insides, so I said, 'We have to DO something about the baron, sir. We're all going to starve to death, AND he took Denzel which is just plain stealing. If our parents aren't going to do anything then it's up to us, isn't it?'

'Why don't we just go up to the castle and punch his lights out, sir?' said Robin.

'Punching the baron's lights out probably wouldn't be a terribly good idea, unless you want to be thrown in the dungeons,' said Gaius.

'Well, what CAN we do then?' said Verucca.

'What about a bit of peaceful protesting?' said Gaius. 'You could make some placards and go up to the castle. You might be able to speak to the baron and tell him how you feel.'

'Will that do any good, sir? I said.

'Probably not, Sedric, but it might make you feel a bit better.'

So we all made placards out of bits of wood with stuff written on them saying how angry we were, except Rubella who said she'd rather jump in a hornets' nest than spend time writing rubbish that no one was going to read, which was fine by me.

My placard said:

Robin's said:

And Verucca's said:

Verucca let Urk share her placard because his

writing isn't very good, and Eg didn't actually do a

placard because he said we'd already used up all the things he was going to say.

Just when we'd all finished and were getting ready to go up to the castle, Rubella said, 'So where are you going now you've made your stupid stick things, then?'

Verucca told her that they weren't stupid stick things and that she should have been listening in the first place.

'They're called placards,' said Robin sniffily, 'and we're going up to the castle.'

'And YOU'RE not coming!' said Verucca quickly.

'I can if I want, can't I, sir?' said Rubella.

'I can see no harm in young Rubella joining you,' said Gaius, 'and young Gert too, of course. After all, this is for the good of the WHOLE village.'

I knew Gaius was right but it was SO annoying.

Chapter Twelve

QUITE A LOT OF SHOUTING AND MARCHING UP AND DOWN

There was an awful lot of complaining on the way up to the castle. It was mostly Urk. He was going on and on about how he was ACTUALLY going to starve to death and did anybody care?

I told him that of course we did but after he had moaned for quite a long time I said that if he WAS going to starve to death could he hurry up and do it because he was getting on my nerves.

My stomach felt like the rats that had been gnawing at it earlier had eaten everything they could and were now playing the drums on my insides.

Rat playing drums

Rubella was the only one **NOT** moaning. She just went on and on about how one day she was going to leave our boring mud— soaked pointless mess of a village where **NOTHING** ever happened and she was going to live in a massive castle and wear expensive clothes and have servants and absolutely **SHEDLOADS** of gold.

Which explained why she wanted to come with us, anyway.

Verucca told Rubella that she was MENTAL because there was totally NO CHANGE that she was ever going to live in a castle.

When we reached the castle everything was very quiet.

Robin went up and banged on the doors. After a while a little high-up slidey window slid back.

A ginger beardy face appeared.

'Yes?' it said.

'We'd like to speak to the baron, please?' I asked as politely as I could.

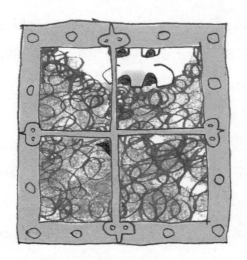

'Have you got an appointment?' said the ginger
beardy face.

Robin asked what an appointment was and the face
said that if we didn't know then we probably didn't
have one and the slidey window slammed shut.

Eg knocked again. The slidey window slid back again.

Eg asked how could we get an appointment and the
face said that we couldn't because the baron was much
too busy to see small pointless peasants and to go

away, and that if we annoyed him again we'd be thrown
into the rat-infested dungeons. Then the slidey
window slammed shut again.

'Rude,' said Verucca.

I'd be lying if I said we weren't a bit disappointed.
We weren't expecting that. Robin said that we
shouldn't give up without a fight and Urk said he really,
REALLY was going to die soon if he didn't have
something to eat.

We decided that if we couldn't get into the castle,
we should try to get the baron's attention by marching
up and down outside and shouting.

We started off by all shouting different things
but that just sounded like a load of random noise.
Then we argued for ages about what we SHOULD
shout. Rubella said she didn't give a monkey's what
we shouted as long as we stopped talking total boring
rubbish and got on with it. So we all held our placards

up high and marched round the castle walls shouting,
'FREE DENZEL AND GIVE US BACK OUR TURNIPS!'

After a few false starts we got a rhythm going.

The trouble was that marching up and down and
shouting and carrying big heavy placards at the same
time is quite tiring when you've had totally nothing to
eat all day, so after a while Urk and Eg stopped and

STOP THE RICH
PEEPEL TAKIN
STUFF FROM
PORE PEEPEL

FREE DENZEL AND
STOP TAKING AR
TURNIPS

GIV SEDRIC BAK
HIS PIG AND
AR TURNIPS TOO

had a rest. Then Robin sat down too and then Verucca and I joined them.

'It doesn't look like anyone is taking any notice of us,' said Urk. 'So that's that then. Who's coming back to the village?'

'What?' said Verucca. 'You can't just give up. What about Denzel? We have to help Sedric get him back!'

'Sorry, Sedric,' said Urk, 'I know he's your mate and everything but the chances of us getting into the castle are about as likely as Mad Warty Edna winning a beauty contest . . . And even if we did get in we'd most likely be caught and thrown into the dungeons and I reckon I'd rather starve to death than be eaten alive by rats.'

'That is just typical!' shouted Verucca. 'Give up at the first teensy-weensy problem, why don't you!'

Urk looked at his feet and mumbled something about not liking small spaces so a dungeon might really freak him out. Eg just groaned and clutched his belly and looked miserable. Rubella said she couldn't care less if my stupid pig got eaten anyway and she and Gert were going back to the village.

'Fine,' shouted Verucca angrily. 'Well, I'm going with Sedric and you wussy wimps can do what you want!'

I don't think Eg and Urk liked being called wussy wimps because after that they decided there was no point in going back to the village anyway as there was nothing to eat so they might as well stay and help me rescue Denzel.

Chapter Thirteen

THE DARK WHICH WAS REALLY VERY VERY DARK

We decided that the best thing to do was to wait until it was dark and then try to sneak into the castle somehow. So we all settled down to wait behind a bush next to the castle wall.

Darkness finally fell. Well, it didn't ACTUALLY fall. Darkness can't do that obviously. It just sort of ARRIVED. Slowly.

I tried hard not to think about what might be happening to Denzel. What if we got into the castle and found him roasting on a spit? Or frying in a frying pan? Or boiled on a plate with an apple in his mouth?

'Did you hear what I just said, Sedric?' said Verucca.

'What?' I said. 'Sorry. I wasn't listening.'

'I said let's play I Spy,' said Verucca.

I started with T for tree. Robin did F for frog which we couldn't actually see but Robin said he DID see before it hopped away so it still counted.

Then it got darker and Verucca did B for bat and Urk did OW for owl. Then we couldn't see anything except M for moon.

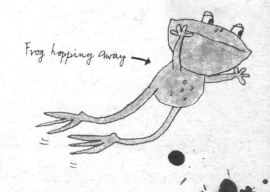

Frog hopping away →

113

I wondered if they could hear our empty bellies gurgling from inside the castle.

Suddenly Eg grabbed my arm and said could I see that pair of fiery red eyes over there in the dark staring at us? I said I couldn't see anything. Robin said it was most probably the Giant Rabbit. Eg said what Giant Rabbit? and Robin said the Giant Rabbit with bulging red fiery eyes and massive dripping jaws and

GIANT RABBIT →
Teeth like knives →
Massive jaws

teeth like knives that breaks into hovels at night and eats children. Eg started to make whimpering noises. Verucca told us to stop being so stupid and that there was no such thing as a Giant Rabbit and that we should be thinking about how we were going to get into the castle to rescue Denzel instead of frightening each other to death.

So we all had a think and came up with:

1. We could find a really long ladder from somewhere and climb over the wall.

2. Borrow a big bear with some really big friends and ask them to break down the castle doors with their massive powerful claws.

3. Sit here in the dark until we turned into skeletons.

Me

Verruca

4. We didn't think of a number 4 because Eg screamed.

'Aaarrggh! Something moved! There's something out there!'

'We're all going to die!' squeaked Urk.

Suddenly we spotted a dark figure moving behind a buttress in the castle wall. It was making a weird jangly noise.

★ **BUTTRESS:** NOUN (A noun is a THING) A structure of stone built against a **WALL** to stop it falling down.

'What is it?' Robin whispered.

'It's the Giant Rabbit!' squeaked Eg.

The dark shape was coming towards our bush.

'Sssshhhh!' I hissed. Everyone was quiet.

How on earth could five people breathing and five empty bellies make so much noise?

The weird jangling noise got nearer.

'OW! Someone's fallen over my foot!' said Urk.

'OH BUM!' said a voice from the darkness, which was attached to a man dressed in a toga who was lying face down on the ground. The bag he was carrying had spilled out coins and jewellery all over the grass. The moon shone on the bag and I read the words: Gluteus Maximus, Genuine Roman Plumber to Royalty and the Filthy Rich.

The man sat up.

'Salve!' he said when he saw us. He looked really guilty as he gathered up all the stuff from the grass and shoved it back in his bag. 'Exempli – er – gratia et cetera – um – pro bona!'

'You can drop all the rubbish Latin,' said Verucca. 'You're not a real Roman at all, are you?'

Dave from Essex pushed the last coins into his bag. 'You won't tell anyone, will you?' he said.

'Not if you show us how to get in to the castle,' said Verucca.

'Behind that buttress,' he said, pointing from where he'd just come.

'What about it?' I said.

'You'll see!' he said as he picked up his bag and set off into the darkness.

Loads of stolen stuff

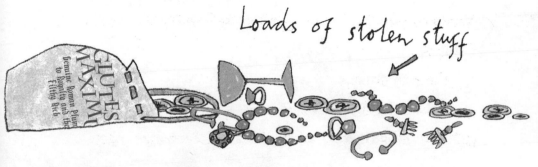

119

I said we should maybe do something about him stealing all that stuff, but Robin said it was OK to steal from the rich as long as you gave it to the poor, and then Verucca pointed out that the baron had stolen OUR stuff so that sort of made it all right.

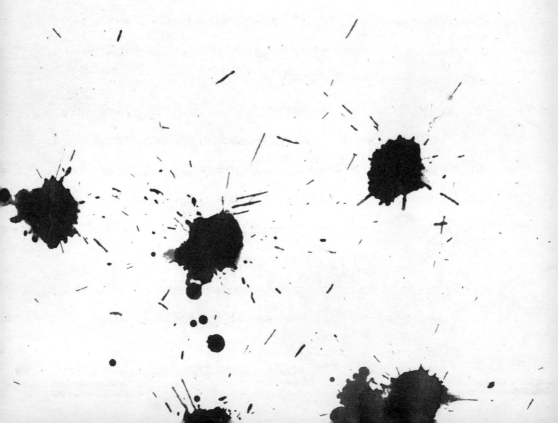

Chapter Fourteen

DUNGEONS AND RATS

Hidden behind the buttress
was a tiny door.

'Well that's a
surprise,' said Verucca. 'Who'd
have thought that when they built
this huge castle with massive
high walls and great big solid

Tiny nipping in and out door.

wooden doors that someone would have said, "I know
what we need here. Let's make a little tiny door for
nipping in and out really quickly?"'

So we nipped through the tiny door and found
ourselves in a long dark damp tunnel.

'I reckon we're near the dungeons,' said Verucca.

'How do you know?' whispered Urk.

'There's a big sign up there on the wall that says TO THE DUNGEONS,' said Verucca.

There were lots of dripping noises and rustling sounds like tiny feet on straw.

'That's rats,' said Urk.

'Would they be the same rats that will eat us alive if Sergeant Hengist catches us?' squeaked Eg.

'You can go back if you want,' I told him.

'No. I'm fine with it.' I don't think he was, though.

We crept along as quietly as we could until we heard footsteps close behind us.

'Some idiot went and left the little nipping in and out door open,' said a voice that was most probably a guard.

'What? Do you reckon someone's nipped out then?' said another guard.

'Dunno. They could've nipped in.'

'That's true. Did you shut it again?'

'Course I did. And locked it. No one's going to be doing any more nipping tonight.'

Oh heck, I thought. We would have to find another way out now.

We reached a door. The voices were coming closer.

'In here, quick!' I whispered and pushed us all through the door and shut it behind us just as the guards went past.

It was very, very dark on the other side of the door. It was so dark that I couldn't even see my own feet.

Then, after my eyes got used to it, I could just see the others. Then I heard squeaking and looked down and saw rat-shaped things moving all over the floor.

We were actually INSIDE a real dungeon!

'AAARGH!' squeaked Eg. 'Something bit me!'

'SSSShhh!' hissed Verucca.

'OWW!' shouted Urk. 'LET ME OUT!'

Heavy footsteps came running back towards us. They had almost reached the door and I was just thinking that I wished my life had been a bit more than *tried to rescue pet pig but got eaten alive by rats in castle dungeons instead* when Robin suddenly whispered, 'What we need here is a diversion! Wait

here till I've gone – then make a run for it!' and before
I could ask him what a diversion was, he pulled his hood
up and slipped through the door.

'There he is!' shouted a guard. 'Get him!'

Chapter Fifteen

DOORS AND DIVERSIONS

As soon as the footsteps had died away, the rest of us crept out of the dungeon, pulling the door firmly shut behind us. Maybe being eaten alive by rats in castle dungeons wasn't going to be my end after all, which was good.

I just hoped it wouldn't be Robin's end either.

'I would DEFINITELY rather starve to death than spend another second in there,' said Urk.

"Right,' I said. 'We need to find Denzel.' Although I didn't have a clue where we should start looking.

'You alright, Eg?' said Verucca.

Eg walked straight past us. He didn't say anything

EG. All staring and weird

and his eyes were all staring and weird. He whimpered a bit, but I couldn't make out any actual words.

We ran along dark damp tunnels that twisted and turned and seemed to go on forever until finally we went round a corner and saw a staircase straight ahead.

It was one of those staircases that go up and up and round and round, so we ran up and up and round and round really fast until I felt a bit sick.

At the very top of the stairs was a door.

Now, the trouble with doors is that you never know

Big fierce dog

Some people ➡ having a **PARTY**

Boiled frogs

what's on the other side until you open them. Unless it's a door you know really well, like the door to your hovel — then you know exactly what's on the other side.

A table and some chairs and your mum, probably.

But a strange door is different. There could be a big fierce dog waiting to bite your leg off, or there could be some people having a party, or a load of witches boiling up some frogs.

'I-i-is s-someone going to open it then?' whispered Eg from the back.

Nobody did. It didn't look as if any of us wanted to so we all stood there in the dark looking at each other, but then Urk farted, so Verucca opened the door quickly before we all choked to death.

Urk's fart →

Urk's farts are killers.

We slipped through into a long corridor. There was nothing much to see in either direction except a lot of naked statues and armour and those metal things that stick out of walls that hold flaming torches. But we could hear footsteps and voices in the distance. They were heading towards us.

'How do I know where he went? He'd finished it, hadn't he?'

It was Sergeant Hengist!

'I'm not sure, sarge. Last thing he said to me was he needed more parts. Now he's gone! I can't find him anywhere, and the baron says her ladyship wants to try it out.'

'Well, he probably got the parts he needed then, didn't he, corporal? Now I suggest you get back to whatever it is you're supposed to be doing and let me have a little tiny bit of PEACE AND QUIET!'

I wondered what all that was about.

But I didn't wonder for long because Sergeant Hengist's great big feet were getting really close now.

'We have to hide!' I said.

'The statues!' hissed Verucca. 'Get behind them!'

So Verucca and Eg hid behind one that was throwing a plate, and Urk and I hid behind one with a branch in her hand wearing some floaty stuff.

'And if you fart I will kill you!' I whispered to Urk.

We all stayed as quiet as mice. Except for Urk who kept sniggering because we were right under the statue's bum. I had to put my hand over his mouth to shut him up.

We could hear the sergeant talking to himself as

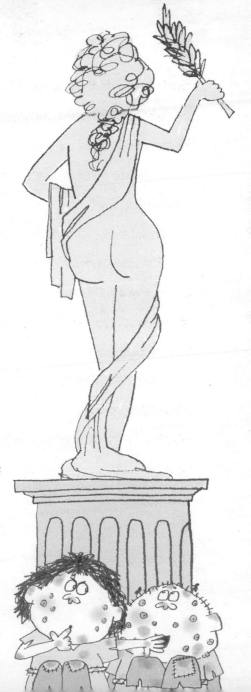

131

he passed right by us. 'That blasted plumber – what's he want to go missing now for? I'll be the one who gets the blame – I get the blame for **EVERYTHING** around here! Gluteus Maximus my foot! Gluteus Stupidus more like . . .' And he carried on mumbling to himself until we couldn't hear him any more.

'What's that?' said Urk, when the sergeant had gone. 'Something's cooking and it smells **AMAZING!**'

We all sniffed. The smell was delicious but it made me remember how starving hungry I was.

HUNGER TRANCE

Delicious sme

Urk followed his nose, and we all followed Urk. Most of us stopped when we got to the top of another long flight of stone stairs where we could hear clattering and banging and lots of shouting coming from the bottom. But Urk didn't. He just carried on walking like he was in a sort of hunger trance. Verucca grabbed his arm to stop him but he tripped and fell.

'AAGGGHHH!'

I could hear him bouncing all the way down to the bottom. It must have **REALLY** hurt.

'There you are, you idiot boy!' shouted someone angrily from the bottom of the

stairs. 'Have you got me that apple yet?'

'That's not the kitchen boy!' said another voice.

'Course it is! Look at him! Gormless, stupid—looking and covered in zits. Who else could it be?'

'IT'S NOT HIM! Our kitchen boy's got loads more zits than this one.'

More zits than Urk! Impossible, I thought.

Urk mumbled something I couldn't hear.

'FOR THE PORK, OF COURSE — STUPID BOY!' Then there was noise like a hand hitting the side of a head.

Pork? Pork was pig, wasn't it?

Denzel! We were too late.

THEY'D ALREADY COOKED HIM!

Chapter Sixteen

A VERY BiG BANG

Denzel was gone.

My faithful friend, cooked and eaten, and I was too late to save him!

I thought I might cry and I didn't want the others to see, so I ran back along the long stone corridor that was all hung with fancy expensive stuff that no one needed. I didn't care any more if I was caught and thrown in the dungeons. Things were as bad as they could possibly be. As well as Denzel being arrested and eaten, we'd lost Robin. He was most probably locked up and being munched by mad flesh—eating rats by now. And Urk was trapped in the kitchens.

AND we were all going to starve to death!

'Sedric! Where are you going?' shouted Verucca.

I slowed down bit. Verucca and Eg caught up with me.

'I'm sorry about Denzel,' Verucca said.

'It's Ok,' I lied. It SO wasn't Ok.

Eg said that it could have been another pig they
were cooking and not Denzel at all but I knew he was
only trying to cheer me up.

'You did all you could, Sedric. No one could've done —' said Verucca, and then she stopped. 'What is **THAT?**' she said.

I turned round and saw a half-open door. Through the door was something huge and shiny. Eg pushed the door open a bit more and he and Verucca went in. I followed, but I wasn't really interested. It could have been the most amazing thing I'd ever seen in my whole life, but I didn't care. All I could think about was Denzel.

As it turned out, it **WAS** the most amazing thing I had ever seen in my whole life. It was absolutely the biggest, weirdest thing **EVER**.

It had to be the Great Big Bubbly Bath Thingy!

Eg was fiddling with everything. I told him to stop before he broke anything because we were in enough trouble already, but he didn't listen.

He opened a tiny door underneath the ladder.

The GREAT BIG BUBBLY BATH THINGY

STEAM →

Pipes ↗

More pipes ↓

Big pile of wood →

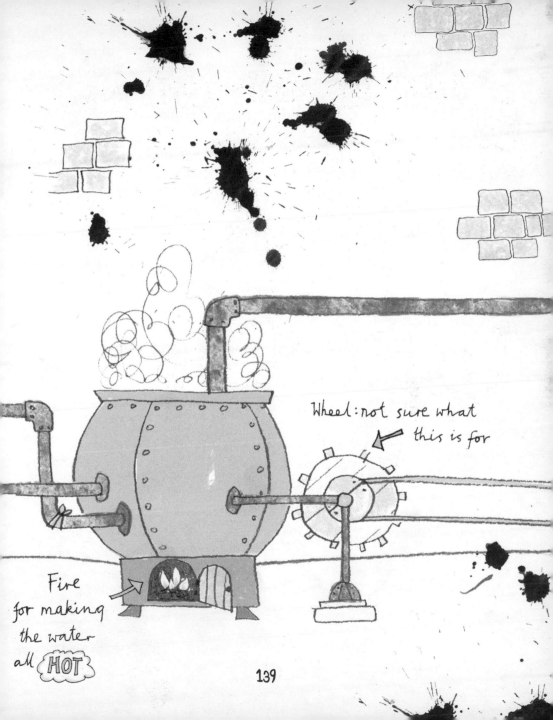

Wheel: not sure what this is for

Fire for making the water all *HOT*

139

There was a small fire smoldering inside and a big pile of wood next to it, so of course he threw all the wood on to the fire. It started to burn really well. Maybe too well actually.

The water in the tank started to bubble, and steam began shooting out of the pipes in all directions, which would have been quite interesting – if I hadn't just wanted to get away from the castle and stop thinking about what had happened to Denzel.

Then we heard voices.

'DENNIS! YOU'RE BEING RIDICULOUS! I AM GOING TO TRY OUT MY NEW BATH AND I DON'T CARE WHAT YOU SAY!!'

'We really ought to wait for Gluteus, my sweet. We don't want any accidents, do we?' said Dennis.

'Of course there won't be any accidents, you silly man! It's a masterpiece of Roman plumbing built to the

very highest standards by an expert craftsman! What can **POSSIBLY** go wrong?'

The baron and Prunehilda had reached the door. We needed to hide quickly!

Eg flapped his arms and turned in circles while Verucca and I looked around for somewhere to hide.

'See, Dennis,' said Prunehilda. She and the baron came through the doors at exactly the same time as we all dived underneath a sort of fancy bed thing draped in cushions and curtains. 'I told you Gluteus wouldn't let us down. He's lit the fire for us already – it'll be lovely and hot.'

I could hear her starting to climb the ladder up to the Great Big Bubbly Bath Thingy. It groaned under her massive weight.

'DENNIS! HOLD MY TOGA!' she ordered.

NOOOO! I just prayed she wasn't naked. I really wouldn't want to see THAT.

The Great Big Bubbly Bath Thingy was making loud

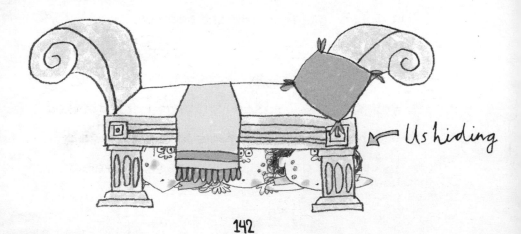

← Us hiding

gurgling noises and steam was puffing out everywhere in huge clouds.

I heard a splash as Prunehilda climbed into the water.

'Mmmmm! Lovely!' she cooed. 'Why don't you join me, Dennis?'

'Oh very well. Coming, my sweet,' Dennis cooed back.

Verucca stuck her fingers down her throat and made gagging noises.

The bubbling noises got louder. More steam was pouring out of the strangely shaped pipes.

Suddenly there was a creak and a crash. One of the pipes had fallen off and landed on the floor.

'DENNIS! WHAT WAS THAT?' squawked Prunehilda, as a burst of steam shot up and

another pipe fell off.

'HENGIST! WHERE ARE YOU?' shouted the baron from deep inside the Great Big Bubbly Bath Thingy. 'AND WHERE IN HADES IS THE PLUMBER?!'

But Sergeant Hengist was nowhere to be seen.

Instead there was another horrible rattling noise and then . . .

Wood and metal flew high into the air. Water poured from everywhere and covered the floor in seconds. More pipes crashed to the floor, things started to catch fire and it was all followed by another massive . . .

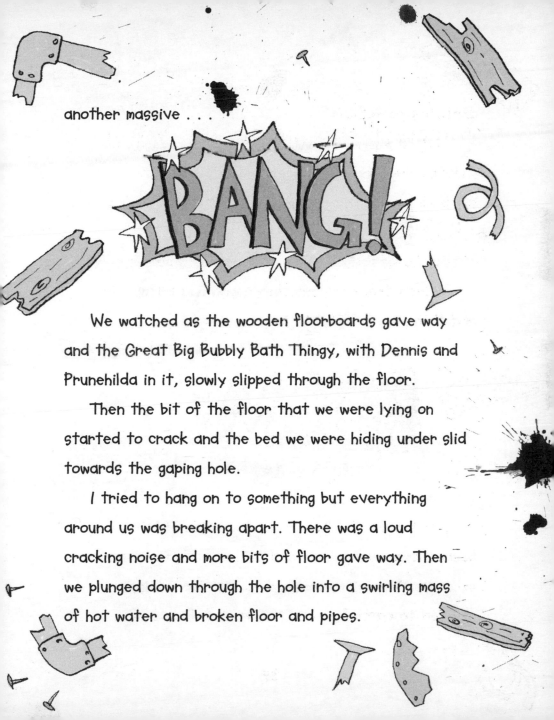

BANG!

We watched as the wooden floorboards gave way
and the Great Big Bubbly Bath Thingy, with Dennis and
Prunehilda in it, slowly slipped through the floor.

Then the bit of the floor that we were lying on
started to crack and the bed we were hiding under slid
towards the gaping hole.

I tried to hang on to something but everything
around us was breaking apart. There was a loud
cracking noise and more bits of floor gave way. Then
we plunged down through the hole into a swirling mass
of hot water and broken floor and pipes.

Chapter Seventeen

IN THE FLOOD

I came up surrounded by water. It was in my ears and up my nose and broken bits of wood and metal were whooshing all around and bashing into me.

Verucca bobbed up next to me gasping for air, then Eg appeared covered in blood.

Even for Eg it was quite an epic nosebleed. The blood swirled around him, turning the bathwater bright red. We seemed to be in the kitchens. People were splashing about everywhere in a panic, trying to rescue

Eg's nosebleed (EPIC) ⟹

all the pots and pans that were floating about. Then, above all the noise of falling wood and pipes and hissing steam, we heard a horrible wailing.

'OH HADES WHAT JUST HAPPENED AM I DEAD I'M GOING TO KILL THAT PLUMBER WHEN I FIND HIM DENNIS DON'T JUST LIE THERE GAWPING LIKE AN IDIOT GET ME OUT OF HERE RIGHT NOW!'

I reckoned that with Prunehilda going on like that, very soon there were going to be soldiers and guards EVERYWHERE, and we would be seen and that would mean we'd end up in the rat-infested dungeons.

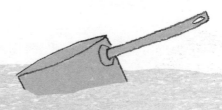

There was loads of stuff swirling all around us in the water. Wooden plates and bowls and pans and spoons and food! LOADS of food! We were in the kitchens! We pretended we were kitchen people to blend in while I grabbed apples and bread and started eating those and Verucca and Eg grabbed some cake that was floating past. It was a bit soggy but they munched it down pretty quickly. There were half-chewed bones and vegetable peelings and mouldy things I didn't recognise and then something I DID recognise . . .

An ugly spiky head all covered in zits and boils.

'URk!'

Loads of FOOD and other stuff

He spluttered a bit and said, 'Oh hi you guys. What are you doing down here? And what's the matter with Eg?'

Eg's nose was still pumping blood.

'Dosebleed,' said Eg.

'Nice one,' said Urk.

I could hear Roger and Norman shouting, 'Don't worry, sire! We'll have you out of there in a jiffy.'

'YOU HAD BETTER, CORPORAL, OR I WILL PERSONALLY HAVE YOU WORKING IN THE KITCHENS FOR THE REST OF YOUR LIFE!'

Urk's ugly spiky head →

'OK, sire, just hang on to us,' shouted Norman.

'Oops! Sorry, sire! You're all slippery! I'll have another go!'

'YOU INCOMPETENT IDIOTS! WHERE'S HENGIST?'

'Here, sire,' came the sergeant's weary voice.

'WHERE IN HADES HAVE YOU BEEN, MAN? GET THESE IDIOTS OFF ME!' shouted the baron.

'It's actually not too bad,' gasped Urk as we waded on through the debris.

'What isn't?' I asked.

'Working in the kitchens. It was well warm and I managed to eat loads. I really enjoyed it – apart from the being hit round the head bit. And the being shouted at bit too.'

There was a creak and a crash as I heard loads more bits of floor falling down into the water.

'OOWWW! GET THIS STUFF OFF ME, YOU COMPLETE MORONS!' shouted the baron. 'CAN'T YOU DO ANYTHING RIGHT?'

'Sorry, sire,' said Roger.

'We're just getting your wife out now, sire. You'll

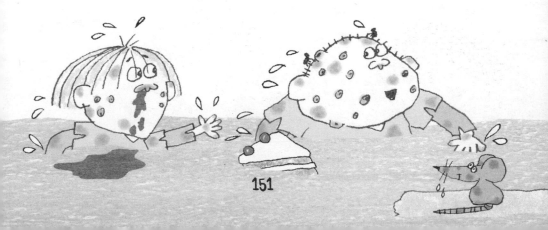

both be right as rain in no time,' said Norman.

Suddenly there was an ear–splitting scream from Prunehilda. 'AARRGGHHH! DENNIS! GET THIS PIG OFF ME NOW AND SOMEONE GET ME MY TOGA!'

Pig?

It couldn't be.

I turned round. Prunehilda was lying TOTALLY NAKED in a pool of broken bits of bath and floor and sitting on top of her with a big happy smile on his face was DENZEL!

Chapter Eighteen

DENZEL AND SOME MORE DARKNESS

Denzel was ALIVE!

He wasn't roasted or boiled on a plate with an apple in his mouth after all! He was ALIVE!

'HENGIST! GET THE PIG!' yelled Dennis.

The sergeant made a lunge at Denzel, but Denzel had already seen me. He looked all excited and he

jumped off Prunehilda and disappeared underneath the swirling water.

'Here's your toga, my lady!' said Roger, shutting his eyes tight as he handed it to her.

Dennis was really shouting at the soldiers now and using words that sounded VERY rude and not what you'd expect from a baron at all. The soldiers were all scrambling around in the water and falling over each other trying to find Denzel.

Verucca, Urk and I were splashing around under the water trying to find Denzel too, while Eg flapped his

Soldiers looking for Denzel

arms and dripped blood everywhere. I told him if he stopped flapping and bleeding quite so much then we'd be less noticeable.

He said, 'I can't help it if I've got a dosebleed, can I?' So I grabbed a piece of screwed-up old parchment that was floating past and handed it to him and told him to hold it on to his nose to mop up the blood.

It helped a bit.

Then Denzel bobbed up next to me, spluttering and choking. I dragged him out of the water and gave him a big hug.

'Can you do all that stuff later?' said Verucca. 'We need to get out of here.'

So I asked Urk if he knew how to get out and he said, 'We need to go up the stairs,' and I said, 'What stairs?' and he said, 'Those stairs,' and I said, 'What? The ones you fell down that are over there on the other side of where the baron and Prunehilda and quite a lot of soldiers are?' and he said, 'Yeah. Those stairs.'

'How are we going to do that?' said Verucca

'We could swim under water,' said Urk.

I pointed out that he couldn't swim.

Dennis - a bit of a funny colour

156

'I know I can't actually SWIM,' said Urk, 'but I can SINK. I'm really good at sinking, which is exactly the same as swimming underwater.'

So we all held our breath and dived down under the water. Urk and Eg came up by the steps. Which was good.

Denzel, Verucca and I came up right in front of Dennis and Prunehilda, which wasn't so good.

Denzel choked and spat out some bath water all over the baron, who went a funny colour.

'HENGIST!' he shouted. 'I THOUGHT I TOLD YOU TO GIVE THAT PIG TO THE COOK! AND WHAT ARE THESE PUTRID PEASANTS DOING IN MY CASTLE?'

And I suddenly felt **REALLY** angry. More angry than I have ever felt in my life before. My head went all hot and before I could stop myself I shouted, 'WHO ARE YOU CALLING PUTRID PEASANTS? THINGS WERE FINE IN OUR VILLAGE UNTIL YOU AND YOUR GREEDY WIFE ARRIVED AND NOW YOU'VE SPOILED EVERYTHING AND WE'RE ALL GOING TO STARVE TO DEATH BECAUSE YOU'VE TAKEN ALL OUR TURNIPS AND I WANT YOU TO KNOW I DON'T THINK THAT'S FAIR!'

Me all hot and **REALLY** angry

158

Everything went very quiet, apart from a few bits of floor that were still dropping from the ceiling. The baron just kept opening and closing his mouth like a fish and the big vein in his forehead started throbbing.

'I think we'd better leave now,' whispered Verucca.

'OK,' I whispered back. I grabbed Denzel and we dived back under the water just as Sergeant Hengist made a grab at us.

We swam and swam until I thought my lungs would burst.

'RUN, SEDRIC, RUN!' shouted Eg, as we surfaced at the bottom of the steps.

I followed the others, and as I ran I noticed a very short soldier racing up the stairs next to us. He had a hood poking out from under his chainmail.

'There's that little toad who broke into the dungeons!' came a voice from the bottom of the stairs.

'ROBIN?'

'Keep going, Sedric!' he shouted. 'There are loads of soldiers behind us.'

'GET AFTER THEM, HENGIST!' shouted the baron from far below, 'AND IF YOU DON'T CATCH THEM, IT'LL BE YOU THAT'S SERVED UP ON A PLATE WITH AN APPLE IN YOUR MOUTH!'

We reached the top of the stairs and burst out into the long corridor. We ran and we ran, and I suddenly felt very hungry and tired and I really, really wanted to be back in my own bed again in my old hovel, and to wake up and find that this had all just been a bad dream.

The castle doors were ahead of us, and they were open!

'COME ON!' I shouted.

Out into the DARKNESS

The only light was from the **MOON**

We ran as fast as we could and threw ourselves through the doors, past the ginger beardy guard who looked **REALLY** surprised, and out into the darkness.

I could hear all the soldiers' great big feet close behind us.

'AFTER THEM!' shouted Sergeant Hengist.

'I CAN'T SEE ANYTHING, SARGE!' shouted Norman.

'OF COURSE YOU CAN'T, YOU IDIOT. IT'S DARK!'

'CAN'T WE FIND THEM

Roger

Norman

Sergeant Hengist

People bumped into each other a lot "OW!"

"Sorry"

IN THE MORNING, SARGE?
THEY'RE ONLY CHILDREN.
THEY HAVEN'T ACTUALLY
HURT ANYONE!' shouted Roger.
 'YOU KNOW SOMETHING
CORPORAL?' shouted the sergeant.

'What, sarge?'
 'YOU REALLY ARE A BIT
OF A GIRL, AREN'T YOU?!'
 'He is REALLY beginning to get on my

nerves,' said Verucca.
 'OOWWW! Stupid tussocks!' muttered

Urk from the darkness.
 'GOTCHA!' said Sergeant Hengist

triumphantly.

 I tripped over Denzel, then Eg tripped

over me. A big burly soldier hauled us both

Urk

to our feet. Then another one grabbed
Robin and Verucca.

But just as Sergeant Hengist
and the soldiers were marching us back
towards the castle, an old familiar figure in a toga
appeared out of the darkness.

'What on earth is going on, sergeant?' he said.

Chapter Nineteen

ESCAPE AND ARREST

'These children are under arrest, not that it's any of your business,' said the sergeant.

'Rude,' said Verucca.

'It's very much my business, sergeant,' said Gaius. 'I am their teacher. Now what exactly are they under arrest for?'

'BREAKING AND ENTERING THE CASTLE, STEALING THINGS —' shouted the sergeant.

'WHAT THINGS?' shouted Verucca. 'WE DIDN'T STEAL ANYTHING!'

'STOP INTERRUPTING!' shouted the sergeant. 'IMPERSONATING A

SOLDIER AND . . . what was the other thing, corporal?'

'Running away, sarge,' said Roger. 'But I really don't think . . .'

'SHUT UP! YOU'RE NOT PAID TO THINK, CORPORAL!'

'Eg! Whatever happened to you?' said Gaius.

'Dosebleed, sir,' said Eg.

'Sergeant,' said Gaius, as he took the bloodstained parchment from Eg and handed him a nice clean hanky to mop up the blood, 'I must protest! These children are innocent!'

'I'm just following orders,' said Sergeant Hengist. 'If you have any complaints you can take them up with the baron later!' And he marched us all back into the castle, slamming the doors behind him.

'What ARE you wearing?' Verucca said to Robin, looking at his chainmail.

'Cool, eh? I found it while I was hiding. Useful for undercover work.'

'Nice one,' said Verucca. 'Except now they'll most probably throw you into the dungeons for impersonating a soldier.'

We were led into the Great Hall.

Dennis and Prunehilda were lying on their beds looking VERY fed up.

A red puddle was collecting on the floor around Eg, whose nose was still bleeding quite a lot in spite of Gaius's hanky. I wondered if that was what he'd be remembered for. Having epic nosebleeds. Then I wondered what I would be remembered for.

I might be remembered for not getting very old.

The baron shouted at us a lot but I wasn't really listening. I was too tired and hungry. I caught the last bit though. The TAKE THEM DOWN TO THE DUNGEONS! bit.

So, it was all over.

We'd tried our best and we'd failed.

We were going to be munched by rats in the dungeons, if we didn't starve to death first. I wondered if it hurt very much being eaten alive. Which bits would the rats start on first?

Anyway. This was it.

THE END.

Me being munched
by RATS

Empty belly →

Chapter Twenty

DENNiS GETS REALLY VERY ANNOYED

'Sire! There's someone here says he needs to speak to you urgently!' said Roger.

'Good grief! What now? Does he have an appointment?' said the baron.

'I don't know, sire. Shall I ask him?'

'OF COURSE ASK HIM YOU STUPID IDIOT!'

'I wasn't aware I needed an appointment, and your corporal is a polite and pleasant young man, and not a stupid idiot at all,' said a voice from outside the door.

'WHO IN HADES ARE YOU?' shouted Dennis.

171

'My name is Gaius,' said Gaius, stepping forward.

'Oh look, Dennis,' breathed Prunehilda excitedly.

'He's a ROMAN!'

'WHATEVER IT IS YOU'RE SELLING WE DONT WANT ANY OF IT!' shouted Dennis.

'I merely require a few moments of your valuable time. I know how tempus can fugit, sire,' said Gaius.

'WHAT IS HE BLATHERING ON ABOUT?' shouted the baron.

'Oooh! It's proper Latin, Dennis,' said Prunehilda excitedly.

'Do shut up, Prunehilda,' said the baron.

Gaius had something in his hand. It was the bloodstained parchment we used to stop Eg's nosebleed. What WAS he doing?

'I have here a document which was found today,' he said, holding it up. 'I believe you know what it is, sire.'

The baron peered at the parchment. A flicker of something crossed his face and he sat up. 'I'VE NEVER SEEN IT BEFORE IN MY LIFE!' he shouted.

'Well, sire, it's the last will and testament of Baron Osric the Incredibly Old. I believe he was your uncle.'

'NONSENSE!' shouted Dennis irritably. 'I SAID I'D NEVER SEEN IT AND I HAVEN'T!'

Roger looked over Gaius's shoulder at the parchment.

'Yes you have, sire. Don't you remember? You gave me and Norm a pile of parchments and you said to take them down to the rubbish and throw them away. You said to make sure we did it properly and I remember thinking at the time it was strange that you'd be chucking all those important parchments out and I said

so to Norm, didn't I, Norm?'

'SHUT UP, CORPORAL!' shouted the baron.

'Allow me to read it out to you, sire,' said Gaius.

So Gaius read Osric the Incredibly Old's last

will and testament. He read a lot of stuff I didn't understand, and I don't think the baron did either.

'Get on with it, man!' Dennis snapped impatiently.

'Very well, sire . . . here we are, right at the end – quite easy to **MISS**, in fact: "And to say a big thank you to the hard-working, loyal and honest villagers of Little Soggy-in-the-Mud, I would like them to have a celebratory feast in my memory to be prepared specially in the castle kitchens."'

'Well, that's not too bad,' said Dennis quickly. 'I'm sure that can be arranged – now, sergeant, take these children **AND** the pig down to the dungeons!'

'There is a little more, sire,' said Gaius quietly.

'Is there? Oh go on then,' said the baron weakly.

'Where is it? Oh yes, here it is: "And as a mark of my respect and thanks I bequeath to the whole village their freedom in perpetuity."'

'What does that mean, sir?' I asked Gaius.

'What it means, young Sedric,' said Gaius, 'is that Baron Osric has given all of you your freedom – forever!'

'Does this mean we get our turnips back?' said Robin.

Eg's noseblood

This is the will of
Osric
The Incredibly Old

Blah, blah, blah – don't really understand any of this stuff – blah, blah – just ignore this bit – it's all in fancy language so just wait for the interesting bit – here it is...

...and to say a BIG thank you to all the HARD-WORKING, LOYAL and HONEST villagers of Little Soggy-in-the-Mud... and as a mark of my respect and thanks I bequeath to the WHOLE VILLAGE their freedom in PERPETUITY

This means forever

Chapter Twenty—one

PRETTY MUCH THE END

After ALL that, Dennis STILL tried to have us taken off to the dungeons to be eaten alive by rats. He was WELL angry about us finding the will and he said it didn't make any difference as we had still broken into the castle, etc. etc.

But then Gaius announced that there was an ancient Roman law that said that trying to get rid of somebody's will was illegal, and that as Dennis had tried to get Roger and Norman to throw Osric's will in the rubbish, he was most DEFINITELY a criminal. Dennis was furious and tried to wriggle out of it but everyone knew what he'd done.

Roman lawyer making up **LAWS** →

So we **DID** get all our turnips back and we finally had our village fair, and it was the best fair **EVER**. The sun shone and everyone was happy.

Robin won the Guess the Weight of the Bucket of Mud competition and Verucca's little brother Burp won a prize for the best fancy dress. He was dressed as a deer. We tied two branches to his head and painted his nose black.

There was singing and dancing and lots of turnip-based food, like turnip turnovers and turnip pies

and turnip cakes and turnip cider and even fancy turnip cocktails with twigs sticking out of them and blackberries stuck on the ends.

It was BRILLIANT.

At the end of the fair Osric's feast arrived. It was delivered to us on our turnip cart and there was food and drink like I have never tasted in my WHOLE life. I ate so much I actually thought I was going to burst.

LITTEL SOGGY-IN-THE-MUD VILLIJ FARE

CES THE WATE OF THE BUKIT OF MUD

OSRIC'S FEAST

Yummy food

Dennis and Prunehilda didn't come down to join us, which I thought was a bit rude. But Roger and Norman came and they had a really nice time.

'That was brilliant you knowing all about that Roman law, Gaius,' I said after we'd finished. 'If you hadn't known about it we'd most probably all be dead by now.'

'Oh I don't think it would have come to that, young Sedric,' said Gaius, smiling. 'But it is remarkable what one can make up when one needs to, isn't it?'

'What – you mean there wasn't **REALLY** an ancient Roman law about throwing wills away?' I said. 'You made it all up?'

182

'Well, there MIGHT have been,' Gaius said happily, 'but I've never actually heard of one. But that must stay strictly between you and me.'

I said his secret was safe with me, and Denzel and I wandered off to eat more food. Then I suddenly remembered Verucca's dream and I realised that everything in it had actually pretty much happened.

Dennis
(feeling VERY grumpy)

But I didn't tell her. She'd have been SO smug.

So everything was good in Little Soggy-in-the-Mud. We had our turnips back, we were all free and happy peasants and Dennis was NOT happy back in his castle.

But I had a feeling that it wasn't the last we had heard of him . . .